MORE TEN-MINUTE ONE ACT PLAYS

JACK B. LEVINE

MORE TEN-MINUTE ONE ACT PLAYS

About the Author

Jack B. Levine is an author, actor, standup comedian, improv performer, and personal storyteller. He has performed on stage and online, appeared on television and radio programs, and presented at the Palace Theater's 2nd Act Series.

Also by Jack B. Levine

Laughing Out Loud: A Memoir

Primer for the Performing Arts

Tales of Mirth and Madness

Parodies and Comedy Skits

Ten-Minute One Act Plays

MORE TEN-MINUTE ONE ACT PLAYS

DEDICATION

This book is dedicated to **Susan R. Levine**, my wife and best friend for fifty years. She has been with me through thick and thin and always is someone I can count on in the best-of-times, worst-of-times, and in-between-times.

SPECIAL THANKS

I want to express a "special thanks" to **Dana Sachs**, who read every draft of every play and provided his thoughtful and helpful comments. Dana was my first director as an actor, has been my mentor, and a very close friend. **Dana Sachs** directed seven of my ten-minute plays in a Zoom performance and my first onstage play, "Skateboards and Blueberry Pancakes". He has truly been an inspiration to me.

MORE TEN-MINUTE ONE ACT PLAYS

Table of Contents

SKATEBOARDS AND BLUEBERRY PANCAKES

<u>Cast of Characters</u>

ALBERT: Male, age 90.

AMY: Female, age 90.

WAITRESS: Female, age 20.

COOK: Male, age 70.

<u>Scene</u>

ALBERT and AMY are seated at a diner.

<u>Time</u>

Present.

SKATEBOARDS AND BLUEBERRY PANCAKES

SETTING: *Diner in mid-morning of a weekday during the winter.*

AT RISE: *ALBERT and AMY, both in their 90's, are sitting at a booth. AMY is knitting. There are no other customers.*

> ALBERT

I wish I hadn't overslept.

> AMY

You were tired, dear.

> ALBERT

I <u>need</u> to eat by seven in the morning.

> AMY

You stayed up late last night.

> ALBERT

I shouldn't have had that popcorn.

> AMY

Nobody forced you to eat it.

> ALBERT

You made it and handed me that bowl.

> AMY

It was supposed to be a little treat.

SKATEBOARDS AND BLUEBERRY PANCAKES

ALBERT

I had indigestion the whole night.

AMY

We'll eat breakfast and go home. You can take a nap.

ALBERT

I have things to do.

AMY

Like what?

ALBERT

It's personal.

AMY

We've been married for seventy years. Nothing's personal.

ALBERT

You're too judgmental.

AMY

What have I ever said to make you think that?

ALBERT

I took up skateboarding –

AMY

Yeah, you just turned eighty when you decided to do that.

ALBERT

I'm young at heart.

SKATEBOARDS AND BLUEBERRY PANCAKES

AMY

You could've killed yourself.

ALBERT

It was a dare.

AMY

You let a teenage boy – what was he? all of fifteen – make a bet you couldn't go down the Town Hall stairs.

ALBERT

What could I do? He challenged me! "Was I a wimp or winner", he yelled out in front of – there must have been twenty people.

AMY

When I got a call from Doctor Jacobson - *(Pause)* You scared the bejesus out of me.

ALBERT

I'm telling you I was doing fine until I hit the second step.

AMY

Well, congratulations, you made step one.

ALBERT

Stop that! Don't be judgmental! I would've made it if someone hadn't yelled.

AMY

That's a lame excuse. Of course, they're going to be yelling: "Fool", "Dummy". Based on the ambulance arriving before you started to try your stupid stunt, I'd say someone called 911 as soon as you were challenged.

SKATEBOARDS AND BLUEBERRY PANCAKES

ALBERT

I was having fun. Feeling good. What's a guy supposed to do?

AMY

You men are alike. You want to show off your manliness. If you ask me, I'm surprised all men haven't killed themselves and left the world with just females.

ALBERT

You're just jealous.

AMY

Let me ask you a question.

ALBERT

Go on.

AMY

I get that you want to be young-at-heart. I admire that. I wish I could be like you at times. But, Albert, you could've killed yourself. Thank goodness it was only broken bones. You would've broken my heart if you left me.

ALBERT

So, what's your question?

AMY

Why don't you enjoy the things you want to do – BUT, for the sake of my sanity – don't put your health and safety at risk.

SKATEBOARDS AND BLUEBERRY PANCAKES

ALBERT

(Long pause. Softly) I guess you're right. I promise – on my honor –
I will. *(Pause)* I love you, Amy. You're the best wife a man could
have.

AMY

Aw. I'll never get tired of you saying how much you love me.

ALBERT

(WAITRESS enters) Oh, finally, we can get some food.

WAITRESS

Hello, folks. I'll be serving you today. At this time in the morning, we
only have two items on the menu. We have eggs – anyway you like
them – with bacon, toast, and coffee. If that's not what you want, we
can make a grilled tomato and cheese sandwich with some potato chips
and pickle. We start serving lunch in half an hour. You can get a full
menu then if you care to wait. So, what's it to be?

ALBERT

What do you want, Amy?

AMY

Oh, I was thinking of pancakes. *(To WAITRESS)* Are you sure the
cook won't make a couple of those? I'd like them with blueberries.

WAITRESS

I'm so sorry. We don't do special orders between the breakfast and
lunch waves. The cook's temperamental. He's especially in a bad
mood today. I wouldn't dare ask him.

SKATEBOARDS AND BLUEBERRY PANCAKES

ALBERT

Young lady, my wife here says she wants blueberry pancakes. This is a diner. I know you serve them, because there's that big sign out front that says, "EGGS, PANCAKES, WAFFLES, AND MORE". So, let's be a good girl and go into the kitchen and tell the cook that my dear wife wants his best blueberry pancakes.

WAITRESS

I'll tell him. But –

ALBERT

Oh, and I'll have the same. Blueberry pancakes, Vermont syrup and butter, and a lot of coffee. And do a couple orders of crisp bacon.

WAITRESS

Don't say I didn't warn you, sir. *(WAITRESS exits)*

AMY

You are so brave! You just took charge. I love that in a man.

ALBERT

I aim to please.

AMY

Do you think we'll get the pancakes?

ALBERT

Look around. We're the only customers. How hard could it be to make a few blueberry pancakes and bacon?

SKATEBOARDS AND BLUEBERRY PANCAKES

AMY

The waitress did say the cook was in a bad mood. *(Pause)* Oh, he's coming now. *(Pause)* I don't think it was a good idea to –

(COOK enters with one
arm in a sling, a patch
on one eye, and a limp.)

COOK

You must be the pain-in-the-ass who insists on a special order – actually two special orders – of blueberry pancakes and bacon. Am I right?

ALBERT

We *(Points to AMY)* are your customers. You know, the people who pay for your food so you can – what the hell happened to you? You look like a truck hit you.

COOK

You!

ALBERT

Look, I only asked for blueberry pancakes and bacon. Let's not make a Federal case of it. Just go back and do some cooking like you're supposed to.

COOK

(Looks at ALBERT) I'm right. You're Albert.

ALBERT

So, what?

SKATEBOARDS AND BLUEBERRY PANCAKES

COOK

You're the one who went down the Town Hall stairs on your skateboard. You're famous!

AMY

He ended up in the hospital.

COOK

(To ALBERT. Excitedly) I was so inspired when I heard about you, that I went out and bought a skateboard. I'm telling you that I spent days trying to learn how to skate. It took a lot of falls and bruises and bandages, but I finally got <u>really</u> good at it. I wouldn't say I was at your level, but at seventy, I made those young snots look up to me.

ALBERT

No kidding. You bought a skateboard. That's fantastic!

AMY

(To COOK) Is that why you're all banged up?

COOK

No. I took up knitting. *(Pause)* Look, I'll be glad to make those blueberry pancakes if you'd do me a big one.

ALBERT

Now, you're talking! What do you need?

COOK

I have my skateboard in the kitchen. I use it to ride back and forth from home. Can you sign it? You know, put your Johnny Hancock on it so I can have bragging rights.

SKATEBOARDS AND BLUEBERRY PANCAKES

ALBERT

Hey, it'll be an honor. Now go back and cook you best blueberry pancakes, and after we eat, we can go out to the parking lot, and I'll teach you a few of my tricks. What do you think of that?

AMY

You'll do nothing of the kind! You promised me, Albert.

COOK

Oh, I won't let him get on my skateboard. He's a whole lot older than me. I'm only seventy. *(To ALBERT)* You've got to be ninety – at least.

ALBERT

Look, toddler, you may be younger than I, but it won't do you any good. I can out skateboard you or anybody else, anytime, anyplace, anyway. You pick the challenge. *(Pause)* We can meet at the Town Hall if you're man enough. What do you say, youngster?

AMY

ALBERT!!!

COOK

(To ALBERT) You're on! Now, let me cook those pancakes/

ALBERT

/ With blueberries.

COOK

Of course. And you're still going to sign my roller board, right? I mean you're doing it <u>before</u> you try to go down those stairs again.

SKATEBOARDS AND BLUEBERRY PANCAKES

ALBERT

I'll sign it before and after. You'll be the one who goes to the hospital.
I'll be getting a bunch of high-fives. Now go do your cooking before I
get too emotional and beat your ass on an empty stomach.

COOK

You are so cool! *(COOK exits)*

AMY

Now, look what you've done!

ALBERT

I got us those blueberry pancakes, you wanted. I got someone who
thinks I'm "The Big Man on a Skateboard". *(Pause)* You've got to be
turned on, Amy. We'll eat our food, then go home and have some fun
in the sack, and then I'll go show this guy and all the others that <u>Albert
is back</u>!

AMY

I'll tell you what's going to happen, Albert. We'll eat and go home,
and you'll be napping within five minutes. When I wake you up, you
won't remember you made this stupid challenge.

ALBERT

I'm going to write a note and put it in my pocket. That way I'll
remember. *(To WAITRESS)* Hey, sweetie, can you bring me a piece
of paper and pencil? I need to write myself a note.

SKATEBOARDS AND BLUEBERRY PANCAKES

AMY

I'll take the note out of your pocket when you're asleep. You'll never remember what you wrote. *(To WAITRESS)* Miss, he doesn't need the paper and pencil. *(To ALBERT)* She's going to bring our meal. You're going to eat it, like a good boy. You're going to sign the cook's skateboard, say you loved the blueberry pancakes, and tell him that you really want to do that challenge, but unfortunately, your wife will beat you up if you do. I think he'll understand.

ALBERT

It's all about me hitting the big 9-0, right? I was primed and ready *(Sighs)* until I became old. I guess my life has passed me by.

AMY

Not completely dear. Here comes the waitress. Eat up. You'll need your strength when we get home. *(Big smile)* If you know what I mean.

ALBERT

Oh, my, oh, my, yes! Yes!

(BLACK OUT)

(END OF PLAY)

BLISSFULLY YOURS

Cast of Characters

JERRY: Male in his early 20's. Newlywed
                                husband of ALICIA.

ALICIA: Female in her early 20's. Newlywed
                                wife of JERRY.

VOICE: Bus driver (speaks without being seen).

Scene

Coach bus.

Time

Present time.

BLISSFULLY YOURS

SETTING:	***Two chairs are positioned downstage center, facing the audience. Lights.***
AT RISE:	***ALICIA, on stage right, in a wedding dress still holding her bouquet in her lap, is looking out the window, JERRY, on stage left, in a tuxedo, is reading a book, for 5 – 10 seconds before he speaks to ALICIA.***

JERRY
(Puts book down on his lap and looks around from a sitting position)
I'm really impressed. This coach is nice. Don't you think?

ALICIA
(Still looking out the window) I guess so.

JERRY
Is something bothering you?

ALICIA
(Turns to look at JERRY) I thought we'd be driving, alone, in your car, on our way to our honeymoon.

JERRY
What could I do? My car wouldn't start.

ALICIA
It's a miracle when it does work.

BLISSFULLY YOURS

JERRY

You're right. I need a new used car. *(Pause)* It was really lucky we could catch a ride on this bus.

ALICIA

We could've rented a car.

JERRY

Honey, this bus gets us to where we want to go for much less.

ALICIA

But we didn't even have a chance to change our clothes.

JERRY

It was either take this bus or wait a week to have my car repaired.

ALICIA

You're right.

JERRY

Are you embarrassed?

ALICIA

I wanted to wear this dress at our wedding, but not here on the bus.

JERRY

You look beautiful.

ALICIA

Thank you, dear. You're very handsome.

JERRY

I can tell something else is bothering you. What is it?

BLISSFULLY YOURS

ALICIA

(ALICIA holds up her bouquet of <u>dandelions</u> which has been laying on her lap) You gave me a bouquet of DANDELIONS!!!

JERRY

Aren't they pretty?

ALICIA

These are weeds!!!

JERRY

(This monologue should be spoken with the bravado of a guy 'who has been caught with his pants down' but is trying desperately to justify his 'little mistake') You've got to know that my intentions were good. You see, I had a lot of stuff on my mind. I wanted to make this the most special day of OUR lives. I'm not saying the rest will be crappy, just that we would be starting our joyous, happy journey, together, forever – you know ''till death do us part'. So, I was in a hurry, and I didn't get to the flower shop until it had closed /

ALICIA

So, you picked these WEEDS for my bouquet.

JERRY

Well, I can explain that.

ALICIA

I'm listening.

JERRY

I realized my 'little mistake'. And I wanted to do the right thing. So, I thought of the beautiful flowers old lady O'Connor grows in the front of her house.

ALICIA

I've seen them. There aren't weeds in her garden.

JERRY

Well, no, you're right, they don't grow in her garden. But you see, when I was about to pick some of those beauties, she came out of her house and asked me what I was doing. I needed to explain why I was there, but I couldn't tell her the truth, so I said, "It was a shame she had some dandelions growing in her yard, and I was going to do the neighborly-thing and pull them out without bothering her."

ALICIA

Did old lady O'Connor buy that malarky?

JERRY

(Proudly) She sure did. That's why you got the beautiful bouquet of dandelions! *(Pause)* And she paid me five dollars!

ALICIA

I guess, it's the thought that counts.

JERRY

(Pause) You know, I was thinking about our first date.

ALICIA

You were incredibly nervous.

JERRY

Yes, I was. And when I am, I talk and talk.

BLISSFULLY YOURS

ALICIA

(This monologue should be spoken with great emotion.) I never told you this. I was happy being single. I only went out with you because my sister said you were desperate. I was just trying to be a nice person. I listened – for HOURS. You told me: What you liked; What you didn't like; What you wanted; What you didn't want. I was so numb at the end of your talkathon that I agreed to see you again, so you wouldn't go on anymore with why I should date you. *(Pause)* We're like the yin and yang.

JERRY

(Sincerely) Am I the 'yin' or the 'yang'?

ALICIA

You could be either.

JERRY

(Thinking) Do you think – um, well, I'm just wondering – maybe we got married a little too fast.

ALICIA

(Thinking the same thing as JERRY) Do you think so? I mean, we only met a week ago.

JERRY

I guess, um, we're different.

ALICIA

I guess we are.

JERRY

You're athletic and love to ski, camp, and climb mountains. All things I hate to do. *(Pause)* I love to play bridge and chess, neither of which you play.

BLISSFULLY YOURS

ALICIA

But I admire the beautiful poetry you write, especially the one you read
to me when you proposed.

JERRY

I wrote that poem before we met. I was picturing the type of girl I
wanted to marry.

ALICIA

(Smiling) So, I was the girl of your dreams.

JERRY

You're beautiful. You have a great smile. You always look nice.

ALICIA

What about the other things? You know, my personality – do you like
that?

JERRY

We're going to get to know each other. It's only been a week.

ALICIA

(Holds up left hand with a string tied around 'wedding finger') Am
I going to get a diamond ring?

JERRY

I thought you said it was cute I used a string 'to tie the knot'.

ALICIA

Well, yes, I did. But I thought you said the real ring was in your other
pants pocket.

JERRY

I did. *(Pause)* It was. *(Long pause)*

BLISSFULLY YOURS

ALICIA

But – what?

JERRY

Um, well, to tell you the truth, the ring is gone.

ALICIA

How did that happen?

JERRY

I brought the pants and some other stuff to the cleaners.

ALICIA

Did you complain to the owner?

JERRY

No.

ALICIA

Why not?

JERRY

I remembered that I had some tissues in the pant's pocket. I'm afraid I must have thrown the ring out with the tissues.

ALICIA

You lost MY diamond ring?

JERRY

Yes, but /

ALICIA

YOU lost my diamond ring?

BLISSFULLY YOURS

JERRY

I really feel badly about it.

ALICIA

You lost my DIAMOND RING?

JERRY

The string has sentimental value.

ALICIA

(Angerly takes off 'string ring' and throws it at JERRY) We're no longer engaged!

JERRY

But we're still married, right?

ALICIA

I guess so.

JERRY

Good. There's no sense throwing away a marriage when you paid fifty bucks.

ALICIA

What are you talking about? The Justice of the Peace is my sister's boyfriend. He didn't charge us anything.

JERRY

You remember. Brad forgot to tell us we needed one more witness besides your sister.

ALICIA

You asked the first person who came into the Town Hall. He was in a rotten mood.

BLISSFULLY YOURS

JERRY

He was there to pay his taxes.

ALICIA

He became upset at us /

JERRY

/ Only when I told him we were taking our vows at Town Hall. He was just being honest. *(Speaking in angry, old man's voice')* "This here wedding is on town property – MY property, as a taxpayer. I pay the electricity, heat, water, cleaning, all of it."

ALICIA

We were only there for ten minutes, so I say, OUR taxes paid for the use of the Town Hall.

JERRY

To calm him down, I gave him fifty dollars.

ALICIA

(Angerly) You idiot! You gave him our honeymoon money. How could you do that? We'll have very little money to do anything. *(Pause)* You don't care. You'll just want to stay in our hotel room and read, write, play chess – with yourself, and watch tv. What am I supposed to do?

JERRY

I never thought of that. *(Pause)* You can learn to play chess.

ALICIA

Boring.

JERRY

We can find a movie on tv to watch together.

BLISSFULLY YOURS

ALICIA

Boring.

JERRY

We can always *(Noticeable wink)* 'do it' *(Smiling)*.

ALICIA

In your dreams.

JERRY

Okay, okay. We'll come up with something fun for you, or better, for both of us, to do together. *(Thinking)*

ALICIA

What are you thinking about? *(Pause)* Don't tell me it's some intellectual game where you prove you're smarter than me. And forget about asking me to try something you like when you won't even agree to go camping or learn how to ski.

JERRY

I don't think putting myself in harm's way is a good idea.

ALICIA

Camping is fun. You're outside, breathing fresh air and seeing nature up close.

JERRY

Bugs, snakes, no air-conditioning, no refrigerator, no microwave, no tv. You can breathe fresh air by going outside and getting the mail. I can buy a National Geographic magazine to see nature.

ALICIA

The food tastes better when you cook it outdoors.

BLISSFULLY YOURS

JERRY

(Sarcastically) Have you ever heard of eating on a deck with a gas grille?

ALICIA

(Crying) I want a divorce!

JERRY

You got it! *(Silence for five beats)*

VOICE

(BUS DRIVER speaks as if using a microphone and is never seen by the audience) May I please have your attention folks. *(Pause)* We have in our midst a newly married couple. *(Pause)* Will you please join me in giving a rousing cheer to the couple in the last row, Mr. and Ms. Jerry and Alicia Anderson!!! *(Pre-recorded sounds of people loudly cheering, followed by shouts of "Speech. Speech. Speech.")*

JERRY

-

ALICIA

-

VOICE

Come on, lovebirds. Don't be shy. We all want to hear from both of you!

ALICIA

(To JERRY softly) You go first, you're the one that loves to talk so much!

BLISSFULLY YOURS

JERRY

Well, um, I not a big public speaker, or anything like that. But I guess I could say a few words. *(Stands and talks to the audience like they're the people in the bus)* Love comes in all sizes. There's 'true love' where you have so much in common. You feel like your spouse is your soulmate, the one and only one you want to be with forever and ever. Only a few people are lucky enough to have that. *(Pause)* Then there's the 'nice love'. I think of this kind of love as where you're comfortable with your spouse. You may disagree occasionally, but you like the person, and they like you. *(Long pause)* And there is a type of love I call "Growing Love". I think most of us have that kind of love. *(Pause)* You see, my wife *(Looks at ALICIA with a sense of caring)* and I are learning about each other, day-to-day. *(Pause)* All of us have flaws. *(Pause)* But we need to have faith in ourselves – in each other – that, if we care enough, love enough, and want it enough – we can work through things, together. *(Pause. A little choked up)* I never realized, until a moment or two ago, that it's too easy to give up. *(Pause. To ALICIA)* There is nothing more that I want than to be with my wife, for the rest of my life. *(Looks at ALICIA for two beats and then sits)*

ALICIA

(Slowly stands) I don't know what to say. *(Pause. Looks at JERRY and then to other passengers, the audience)* We married young, and we married quickly. One week from our first date to our wedding. *(Pause. Pre-recorded sounds of grasps and murmuring)* I was enjoying being single. Dating a lot. But I went out on a blind date because my sister thought I'd like Jerry. *(Pause)* My first impression was he talked too much. *(Pre-recorded laughter from other passengers)* But I can, too. So I didn't think it'd be a problem. *(Pause)* But then we both realized how different we were. *(Pause)* But there was this chemistry. And it made us feel close. Connected, I guess you could say. *(Pause)* They say, "Opposites attract". *(Looks at JERRY)* You know, we're going to make it work. Aren't we?

BLISSFULLY YOURS

JERRY

(To ALICIA. Softly) Yes, we are. *(ALICIA sits. ALICIA and JERRY kiss. Pre-recorded clapping and cheering)* I love you.

ALICIA

I love you, too.

VOICE

Let's hear a big cheer for our newlyweds!!! *(Pre-recorded clapping and cheering)*

ALICIA

Is the divorce off?

JERRY

What do you want?

ALICIA

I don't know. *(Pause)* What do you want?

JERRY

Can we try again? I mean, can we be married and see if we can make it work?

ALICIA

I guess so.

JERRY

You don't seem sure.

ALICIA

Are you sure?

BLISSFULLY YOURS

JERRY

As much as you are.

ALICIA

(Pause. Thinking) We look good together.

JERRY

Your sister is going to marry my best friend.

ALICIA

So, we're connected, one way or the other.

JERRY

Yes, one way or the other.

ALICIA

Will you buy me a diamond ring?

JERRY

Right after I pay for my new used car.

ALICIA

Will you at least try to go camping?

JERRY

(Thinking) Yes. But you have to learn how to play chess.

ALICIA

(Thinking) Do I have to beat you.

JERRY

No.

ALICIA

Are you ready for a lifetime of me?

JERRY

Oh, baby, I am! *(Pause)* Do you want to open a flower shop? We can call it, "Dandelions Forever". *(ALICIA gives a light punch to JERRY's arm, then JERRY and ALICIA kiss passionately)*

(BLACK OUT)

(END OF PLAY)

BONDS THAT NEVER BREAK

<u>Cast of Characters</u>

ALEX ROSS: Forty-five-year-old male. Brother of CHARLES.

CHARLES ROSS: Forty-year-old male. Brother of ALEX.

<u>Scene</u>

Coach bus.

<u>Time</u>

Present.

BONDS THAT NEVER BREAK

SETTING: *Two chairs are positioned downstage center, facing the audience. Lights.*

AT RISE: *Charles, on stage right, the side with a window, is looking out the window, Alex, on stage left, is reading a script and making notes on it, for 5 – 10 seconds before he speaks to Charles.*

ALEX

(Looks up from script, watches his brother for two beats, and speaks) I have a bag with a couple of sandwiches.   Are you hungry? *(CHARLES is loss in thought. ALEX gently touches CHARLES to get his attention)* A sandwich will do you some good.

CHARLES

(Still looking out the window) I love looking at the scenery. It looks so beautiful. *(Turns to look at ALEX)* Do you remember the time dad took us camping?

ALEX

(Thinking)   Are you talking about the first anniversary of mom's death?

CHARLES

I always wondered why dad picked that day.

34

BONDS THAT NEVER BREAK

ALEX

He thought it would be something mom would've wanted us to do.
(Pause.) She never could stand us being morose.

CHARLES

We certainly had a few laughs.

ALEX

Dad was trying so hard to act like he'd been on thousands of camping
trips.

CHARLES

Unless he went camping as a boy – and I truly doubt that – this was his
first – and only, I might add – 'walk in the woods'.

ALEX

(Remembering) Dad was trying to assure us that setting up a tent,
building a campfire and cooking, all would be a 'piece of cake'.

CHARLES

As I remember, he bought the 'best budget family tent'. The salesman
assured dad that he could set it up, without any trouble, in less than ten
minutes.

ALEX

(Laughing) Poor dad. He took ten minutes to read the instructions,
thirty plus minutes to find 'the perfect spot', and – if memory serves
me – it took over two hours, with multiple fits and starts, and the tent
still laying on the ground.

CHARLES

Dad swore. It was the first time I ever heard him do that.

ALEX

Mom would never have tolerated it.

BONDS THAT NEVER BREAK

CHARLES

He looked up and immediately apologized.

ALEX

I'm glad you suggested we could set up the tent by ourselves.

CHARLES

I could see the relief on dad's face. Although he acted like it was no big deal for him to get the tent up – if he tried 'just one more time'.

ALEX

Dad had no trouble with the campfire. *(Pause)* In fact, the steaks were great!

CHARLES

(Quiet for a moment. Sighs) We were laughing so hard that I didn't realize dad actually started to cry, not from the laughing, but /

ALEX

/ The roasting of marshmallows will always remind us of mom. She loved to eat them.

CHARLES

Marshmallows and popcorn, our Friday night snack while we watched a movie, together as a family.

ALEX

I know mom loved the romantic comedies best of all. What do you think dad liked?

CHARLES

Anything mom picked he said was a wonderful choice.

ALEX

(Looks at wristwatch) We should arrive in about two hours.

CHARLES

I suppose so. *(Long pause)* How's your script coming along?

ALEX

It's almost done.

CHARLES

Can I read it now?

ALEX

Not yet. I want to finish the last scene.

CHARLES

What's your play about?

ALEX

Us. Our family.

CHARLES

(Pause) So, I'm thinking your last scene will be about the family gathering we're going to.

ALEX

Yes. But more than that. *(Long pause)* Do you remember our first dog? His name was Fritz. You were only one year old when we had to put him down. It was so sad.

CHARLES

I wish I did. I was too young. *(Pause)* Dad liked to talk about him.

ALEX

I was only six. But I clearly remember Fritz sitting in the back seat of our car – while I was strapped in my car seat – he would lay his head on dad's right shoulder as dad drove the car.

BONDS THAT NEVER BREAK

CHARLES

I remember Tucker. He was a little too aggressive. Barked a lot. But he was fun to play with.

ALEX

Do you remember how I pleaded for a pony?

CHARLES

Yes, I do. We went to the church fair on the green, and you got to ride the pony. You couldn't stop talking about it.

ALEX

Dad promised to take us riding on a pony the next year when they held their next fair.

CHARLES

You lost all interest in ponies in about two months. *(Pause)* Roller coasters were your new thing. *(Laughing)* I remember you 'negotiating' with dad about giving up wanting a pony and instead having dad build a roller coaster in our backyard.

ALEX

Dad said nothing but had his mouth wide open, but mom chimed in and suggested we go to the amusement park on Sunday.

CHARLES

Dad and I went on the big one, but you refused. "It's too fast for me!", you said.

ALEX

But while you and dad road that monster, mom and I went and got some cotton candy.

CHARLES

I don't know why, but I never liked cotton candy.

BONDS THAT NEVER BREAK

ALEX

But you and dad got your ice cream.

CHARLES

Rainbow Delight, which was my favorite back then.

ALEX

Dad always got vanilla with hot fudge, no whipped cream or cherry.

CHARLES

Mom had the same as dad.

ALEX

(Long pause) They genuinely loved each other.

CHARLES

And us.

ALEX

Yes, and us, too. *(Long pause)* Do you think dad's with mom?

CHARLES

I'm certain of it.

ALEX

It's nice the family is getting together for a memorial service.

CHARLES

Yes. *(Long pause as CHARLES looks out the window. CHARLES starts to cry)*

ALEX

(Recognizes CHARLES is tearful and sad and gently touches him on the shoulder as CHARLES continues to look out the window) Let's eat those sandwiches I made.

BONDS THAT NEVER BREAK

CHARLES

(Still looking out the window) I'm not really hungry, right now.
(Turns and looks at ALEX)

ALEX

Are you okay? You look tired.

CHARLES

I'm fine. It's just a lack of sleep.

ALEX

It's hard. I know.

CHARLES

I started clearing out my closet last night to make some room, and I
ended up finding a tin box – it was the one mom kept her personal stuff
in.

ALEX

Oh, yeah, I remember. You never looked inside of it before last night?

CHARLES

I couldn't. But I knew someday I would want to find out what mom
kept.

ALEX

What did you find?

CHARLES

*(CHARLES reaches into his pocket and hands ALEX an old photo.
ALEX looks at it)* I think you were ten or eleven.

ALEX

It was my tenth birthday.

BONDS THAT NEVER BREAK

CHARLES

Mom thought it would be fun.

ALEX

(Pointing to photo) Look at that! What were you doing?

CHARLES

I had my mouth open because you looked like Frosty the Snowman.

ALEX

Mom asked me to open up the flour and pour it –

CHARLES

All over you?!?

ALEX

Mom started to laugh so hard –

CHARLES

You got to admit it was funny.

ALEX

I didn't even realize dad had come into the kitchen and took the photo.

CHARLES

I don't remember why he was home.

ALEX

He took a leave of absence.

CHARLES

To be with mom?

ALEX

Yes.

CHARLES

Did he help?

ALEX

(Imitates father) "Men don't do women's work." *(Pause)* We were having too much fun to care. You know, some of the best times we had as kids were with mom. She knew how to make us feel good about ourselves. Like "Home Kitchen Disasters!" – that could be a fun reality show – if mom were running the show.

CHARLES

She could brighten up just about anything.

ALEX

Yes, she could.

CHARLES

She said something about needing eggs in the batter -

ALEX

The operative word was 'in' – like in the batter.

CHARLES

It was only four eggs before mom took them away from me.

ALEX

It's funny how you can remember the number of eggs after about thirty-five years.

CHARLES

I thought she would've found it funny.

BONDS THAT NEVER BREAK

ALEX
Oh, sure, eggs splattered on the kitchen floor - and me!

CHARLES
You were a sight to behold.

ALEX
I thought when mom slipped and fell –

CHARLES
She was laughing and using her hands to spread the eggs all over me!

ALEX
Mom sure knew how to laugh.

CHARLES
She wasn't laughing when I climbed up on the stool.

ALEX
You could've killed yourself.

CHARLES
I was only trying to be helpful.

ALEX
Chocolate chip cookies don't go in cakes.

CHARLES
You're so conventional.

ALEX
What about my idea, putting a couple of firecrackers on top of my cake?
It would've been spectacular.

BONDS THAT NEVER BREAK

CHARLES

I must admit, I would've loved to see it – imagine dad saying we needed to sing the "Happy Birthday" song, and then lighting what he thought were candles and having the – F I R E C R A C K E R SSSSSSSSSS!!! going off.

ALEX

Then mom left to get more eggs.

CHARLES

She was laughing when she left –

ALEX

But she wasn't too happy when she came home.

CHARLES

I am not taking the blame for the fire. I was only five. You were the adult in-charge.

ALEX

I was just trying to help.

CHARLES

Mom said to put the oven on.

ALEX

Yeah, I know. 350 degrees.

CHARLES

When the smoke alarm went off -

ALEX

I yelled "Fire!!!" and dad came downstairs to see what was up. I forgot to check the oven. *(Pause.)* You like blaming me, don't you?

BONDS THAT NEVER BREAK

CHARLES

It's like my mission.

ALEX

Dad must have called 911. *(Pause.)* He never said anything. I think he was happy to see mom happy and us having a great time with her. We needed that. Mom did, too.

CHARLES

I think we got our sense of humor from her. Don't you think?

ALEX

No doubt about it.

CHARLES

I wish we could make a cake with mom now.

ALEX

I think we just did.

CHARLES

(Long pause) You said, you're going to put in the last scene something about the memorial service for mom and dad. You also said there would be "more than that". What did you have in mind?

ALEX

(ALEX becomes emotional as he speaks) You won't remember this, but it is my fondest memory. It was the day after you were born. I had just turned five the week before, and mom had told me that you were the 'special present from God' for my birthday and the rest of my life. *(Choking up)* I got to come into the hospital room, with mom sitting up in bed and holding you, while dad sat in a chair with the biggest smile I've ever seen him have. *(Pause)* Mom asked me if I'd like to hold "your baby brother".

BONDS THAT NEVER BREAK

CHARLES

You never told me about this.

ALEX

(Long pause, holding back tears) There you were. So small – and I must say, you were more interested in getting fed by mom than being in my arms. *(Long pause, then with a release of deep love towards his brother)* But I knew – I just knew – we would always be close.

CHARLES

Do you want to know what my fondest memory is?

ALEX

Baking a cake with mom.

CHARLES

I mean, of you and me.

ALEX

(Long pause, thinking) I'm not sure.

CHARLES

Do you remember when I rode my first bike?

ALEX

Oh, yes, I do! You got going okay, but somehow you managed to run right into Old Man Donovan's fence. I thought you might have killed yourself.

CHARLES

I really got banged up. Crying and screaming at the top of my lungs.

ALEX

How can that be your fondest memory?

BONDS THAT NEVER BREAK

CHARLES

You were the one who came running. You told me not to worry, everything was going to be alright. *(Choking up)* You said, you'd always be there for me.

ALEX

It never crossed my mind to do anything else.

CHARLES

(Pause. Sighs) We'll always miss mom and dad.

ALEX

Yes, I know.

CHARLES

But we will always have each other.

ALEX

Yes, I know.

CHARLES

I'm hungry. Can I have one of the sandwiches you made?

ALEX

Sure. *(Reaches down and picks up sandwich bag and hands a sandwich to CHARLES)* What do you think mom and dad are eating now? *(Laughing)* I'm sure dad would be eating now because it's noon.

CHARLES

There's no doubt in my mind. They're eating hot fudge sundaes with no whipped cream or cherry.

BONDS THAT NEVER BREAK

ALEX
(Looking up and laughing) No question about it!

(BLACK OUT)

(END OF PLAY)

LOVE AND OTHER AILMENTS

Cast of Characters

WILLIAM JENKENS: An older man.

TEDDY BURNHAM: A younger man.

Scene

Livingroom.

Time

Present.

LOVE AND OTHER AILMENTS

SETTING: *Living room.*

AT RISE: *WILLIAM is seated and reading a newspaper.*

WILLIAM

(Looking at newspaper and reading to himself) "Couple wed fifty-years". Boy, does that guy look like he's been in pain for most of that time. I'd bet a buck that she wears the pants in the family. Their marriage was probably the definition of a tainted love. *(TEDDY enters and WILLIAM looks up from newspaper)* Oh, it's you. Come sit down. Take a load off your feet.

(TEDDY sits.)

WILLIAM (Continued)

Well, glad to see you, Teddy. You're looking bright and cheery.

TEDDY

I am sir. How are you doing?

WILLIAM

Surprisingly good for an old guy. Can't complain.

TEDDY

Your wedding anniversary party was really nice.

WILLIAM

I'm glad you liked it.

TEDDY

You know, Mr. Jenkins, I've been going with Joyce for almost two years.

LOVE AND OTHER AILMENTS

WILLIAM

And you're both happy. *(Teddy smiles and nods)*

TEDDY

Yes, sir, very much. *(Pause)* That's why I came over to speak to you.

WILLIAM

Of course, I figured as much. Joyce has been dropping hints for the last few days.

TEDDY

You and Mrs. Jenkins are an inspiration.

WILLIAM

Let me ask you a question. Is there anything you don't like about Joyce?

TEDDY

Oh, no, sir, she's perfect.

WILLIAM

I thought the same thing when I met Joyce's mother.

TEDDY

If you're thinking of telling me Joyce isn't perfect –

WILLIAM

Oh, no. I agree my daughter is perfect. But you might – no, you will – find certain things – over time – will get on your nerves.

TEDDY

I can't imagine –

LOVE AND OTHER AILMENTS

WILLIAM

You like football. *(TEDDY nods)* You're watching the Super Bowl. Your team is up by three points. There is thirty seconds to go. Are you getting the picture? *(Pause)* The other team is on the seven-yard line. As I said, there is only thirty seconds left on the clock. *(Pause)* And your wife nonchalantly picks up the remote control and switches to the Home Shopping Channel.

TEDDY

We don't watch TV.

WILLIAM

You do go to the bathroom? *(TEDDY nods)* You like to keep your things in a certain drawer. *(TEDDY nods)* Forget it. She will take over – ALL the drawers - and put lotions, shampoos, lipsticks, scented soaps, hair dryer, combs, brushes – the whole shebang of <u>her</u> stuff in <u>every</u> <u>single</u> <u>drawer</u>. And where do you think your stuff will go? *(TEDDY is silent)* In a box, in a closet. So, you'll need to pull out the box and get your stuff whenever you need it.

TEDDY

But you have two bathrooms. Why don't you just use the other bathroom?

WILLIAM

That's <u>not</u> my point! You will become like a second-class citizen. (Pause.) Here's one for you. I tell her to buy Toasty Flakes – my favorite cereal. It's crunchy with just the right amount of sugar. So, get this. She eats <u>my</u> cereal. Do you see what I mean?

TEDDY

She obviously has the same taste as you.

LOVE AND OTHER AILMENTS

WILLIAM

She does the shopping. She could pick up whatever cereal she wants.
If she wants Toasty Flakes, well, she should buy a box for herself. I
wouldn't touch her cereal. I <u>respect</u> her property.

TEDDY

I like eggs for breakfast.

WILLIAM

You have a car. *(TEDDY nods)* You've got tools. *(TEDDY nods)*
Well, think about this. You need a wrench. You go and look for it.
Nowhere to be seen. So, you think to yourself: my wife would have
no need for a wrench. But, just for the sake of checking all possibilities,
you ask. *(Pause)* She borrowed it to bang in a hook to hang a little
banner she bought – "HAPPINESS HERE!". She used a wrench. Who
does that?

TEDDY

Oh, yes, I saw the banner. It's nice.

WILLIAM

You probably never used a wrench in your life so you're not seeing my
point. Let me try another one. She gets a whole new hairdo and
coloring. She comes home with a big smile. I say, "What's for
dinner?" She gets grouchy and tells me I should say something about
her hair. So, I'm kind of defensive. You know, it's like she's attacking
me. So, I calmly and nicely say, 'You look good." She kisses me. I
think things are now okay. So, I say – not in any huffy, puffy way,
"What're you making for dinner."

TEDDY

I like to cook, so we wouldn't have that problem.

LOVE AND OTHER AILMENTS

WILLIAM

You're going to be the perfect husband. I suppose you'd be okay with the toilet paper being put on the wrong way; or a dozen or so shoes being left out by the bed, so you end up tripping over them if you're not careful; or – now listen to this – she doesn't laugh at my jokes!

TEDDY

Um, I'm sure she is laughing inside.

WILLIAM

Oh, if you're going to use that logic – I'm thinking how beautiful she's looking – in my mind – so why should I get a lot of grief for not expressing myself out loud?

TEDDY

I never thought of that. You're making a real good point. There was a time Joyce got upset I didn't say anything about a new dress she was wearing.

WILLIAM

There you go! So, what did you do?

TEDDY

I apologized and said she looked beautiful.

WILLIAM

But what if you thought it and didn't say it? I bet there would've been blowback.

TEDDY

Do you think so? *(WILLIAM nods and encourages more from TEDDY)* And, as I think about it, Joyce does have a habit of finishing my sentences a lot of times.

LOVE AND OTHER AILMENTS

WILLIAM

You see! That bothers you – right? – a lot.

TEDDY

No. On the contrary, I appreciate her helping me get what I'm trying to say right.

WILLIAM

You've got it bad. Sort of like me in the beginning. *(Pause)* Oh, now, I've got it. We were on a camping trip. We had a two-person tent. I put it up and made it really comfortable. We ate and got settled in the tent. Then it rained – I mean, it rained really hard. Low and behold, the tent had a small leak. It dripped. So, what does my wife say? "Can we switch places?" She wants me to sacrifice my goodnight's sleep. "Can you be a gentleman?" says she. What was I supposed to do?

TEDDY

I've got some great stuff to stop small leaks in tents. I'll loan it to you the next time you go camping.

WILLIAM

Is there anything – anything, big or small – that would get under your skin about your future bride?

TEDDY

(Thinking) Oh, yes, Joyce and I went camping. There were a lot of mosquitoes. Joyce forgot to bring the bug spray.

WILLIAM

(Hopefully) Did you have a big fight?

TEDDY

Actually, no. *(Somewhat embarrassed)* We snuggled a lot under the covers.

WILLIAM

So, you came here I assume to ask me the big question.

TEDDY

Yes sir. I did come to speak to you. I love your daughter with all my heart. She's my soulmate. I think we're like you and Mrs. Jenkins. Joyce and I want to get (married) –

WILLIAM

I've got the be-all-to-end-all to tell you. Do you want to have kids?

TEDDY

We hope to –

WILLIAM

We had Joyce. She's been an absolute delight from the first day. I couldn't be happier with her. But we stopped at one. My wife expected me to change Joyce's diaper now and again. *(Looks carefully at TEDDY)* Now, this is not a small thing. You've got to be committed. I'm telling you that babies are fine until they poop. After that, you'll love 'em again. But while you're changing their diaper – you'll find out.

TEDDY

Joyce wants at least three kids. I like kids, too.

LOVE AND OTHER AILMENTS

WILLIAM

Oh, right, your generation has disposal diapers. We used cloth diapers. They had the throwaways, but her mother wanted to use cloth. I guess it's better on the behind.

TEDDY

I do love your daughter. I know there will be things that will come up. But it's just part of life, I guess. *(Pause)* Joyce and I will be devoted parents. We will give you grandchildren.

WILLIAM

Oh, I see where this is going. I – I mean we – will become your go-to babysitters. And if I know my wife, it's going to be payback – big time – and I'll be the one who has to change <u>all</u> of the diapers.

TEDDY

We'll wait until your grandchildren are potty-trained.

WILLIAM

No, no, no. That's not a good solution. You'll bring them over but make sure they have a clean diaper on. And you'll time it, so you'll get back here before – well, you know.

TEDDY

Of course. You can count on me, Mr. Jenkins. *(Nervously)* So, do you give us your blessing to get married?

WILLIAM

Sure. Why not? Joyce will move out and I'll get to use her room – oh, who am I kidding? Mrs. Jenkins will take over the room for her sewing.

LOVE AND OTHER AILMENTS

TEDDY

I think it's up to Joyce how she wants to decorate our house of the future. She can figure out how each room is used. I don't mind. If she's happy that's all I care about.

WILLIAM

(Mumbles) He's drunk the Kool Aid. *(Louder)* So, you don't care? You're okay with whatever Joyce does.

TEDDY

Oh, yes, Joyce has great taste. She's going to make our future home into something special.

WILLIAM

You know, Teddy, I like your attitude. You'll makes Joyce happy, and you'll wonder why you end up taking a lot of tranquillizers.

TEDDY

I do have a question, sir.

WILLIAM

Yes?

TEDDY

What's your secret?

WILLIAM

What do you mean?

TEDDY

You've lived with the same woman for many years. Most marriages end in divorce. What makes a good marriage?

LOVE AND OTHER AILMENTS

WILLIAM

Beats me.

TEDDY

So, are you saying you just go with the flow? It'll work out if the two of you love each other. Is that the secret?

WILLIAM

Have you ever heard of 'tainted love'? *(TEDDY shakes his head)* Well, it's a love that's so deep and true and honest that you cannot possibly imagine something happening to end it. But it does, you see. This great love ends. Do you know why it ends?

TEDDY

No sir.

WILLIAM

Listen up, Teddy. This is going to be the most important thing I'm ever going to tell you. *(TEDDY is listening intently)* When Mrs. Jenkins said, "I do", there was no mention that she was going to turn off my football game with thirty seconds left to go, use every single drawer in the bathroom, eat my cereal, use my wrench as a hammer – none of that! All GOOD reasons to make our love tainted.

TEDDY

I can't wait to marry your daughter.

WILLIAM

Neither can I.

(BLACK OUT)

(END OF PLAY)

MY PARADISE ISLAND

<u>Cast of Characters</u>

RAYMOND: Male in his 60's.

BARBARA: Female in her 60's.

VOICE #1:   Male.

VOICE #2:   Female.

<u>Scene</u>

A small island located someplace in the middle of the ocean.

<u>Time</u>

The present.

MY PARADISE ISLAND

<table>
<tr><td>SETTING:</td><td>A small island in the middle of the ocean. Lighting and soft background sounds may be used to indicate small waves lapping onto the shore. The stage should be totally bare except for one palm tree with one coconut.</td></tr>
<tr><td>AT RISE:</td><td>RAYMAND and BARBARA are standing beside their two suitcases and looking at the ocean through the fourth wall.</td></tr>
</table>

[Playwright's notes to Director: There are three notes in boldface, italics within the play. These are 'fun facts'. In past performances, these have been read offstage or prerecorded.]

RAYMOND

Beautiful. Don't you think? You always wanted a place by the ocean.

BARBARA

Yeah, I did. I never thought it would come true.

RAYMOND

It took a little longer than I expected.

MY PARADISE ISLAND

BARBARA

(BARBARA takes RAYMOND's hand) You worked hard. You kept your promise to me.

RAYMOND

You're the best. I've been so lucky for all these years.

BARBARA

Forty years.

RAYMOND

Right. Today's our fortieth wedding anniversary. You're as beautiful today as you were back then.

BARBARA

You're making me blush. *(Pause)* Are you hungry?

RAYMOND

I'm famished.

BARBARA

How about we do takeout?

RAYMOND

Yes, of course. You shouldn't have to cook on our anniversary.

BARBARA

What do you feel like eating?

RAYMOND

(Looks around and stares at the coconut tree) I know. Let's get the same meal we had on our first date. Remember?

MY PARADISE ISLAND

BARBARA

How can I forget?

RAYMOND

(RAYMOND takes a cell phone out of his pocket and dials) Hello?
I'd like to order lobster and steak with a bottle of your best wine.
(Pause) Salad, baked potato, fresh bread. *(Pause)* Oh, we'll need a
table, couple of chairs, plates, wine glasses, and silverware. *(Pause)*
What?!? You don't rent or sell furniture or tableware. Well, we need
it. So, please make an exception. I'll be giving a <u>really good</u> tip.
(Pause) I don't care how much it's going to cost me. It's our fortieth
wedding anniversary. *(Pause)* Yes, I'll wait so you can get your
manager.

BARBARA

Honey don't get upset. I could cook – *(RAYMOND puts up his hand
to stop BARBARA from talking)*

*[Playwright's note to Director: The cell phone can work on this
island in the middle of the ocean, because the palm tree is a Super
Antenna Tower, SAT]*

RAYMOND

(RAYMOND speaks into his cell phone) Yes, I'm the one wanting the
furniture and tableware. I'm not talking about buying it, just renting it
– for one meal. *(Pause)* I know it's unusual. You do put the customer
first. Right? *(Pause)* Well, yes, I know it's going to cost me a pretty
penny, but it's our wedding anniversary. *(RAYMOND smiles at
BARBARA)* Well, thank you, sir. So, how long will it take to deliver
it? *(Pause)* My Paradise Island. *(Pause)* Yes, that's right. We're on
My Paradise Island. I'm sure you've heard of it. *(Pause)* No? Are
you new to the area? *(Continued)*

RAYMOND (Continued)

(Pause) I'm not trying to be rude. I just thought everybody would know about this beautiful place. *(Pause)* Well, take out a map. We're surrounded by water, in the ocean. It can't be hard to find. *(RAYMOND looks stunned)* He hung up!

BARBARA

We're new to the neighborhood, dear. Nobody is going out of their way for someone they don't know.

RAYMOND

I guess you're right. I just thought the guy would've wanted to make our anniversary special.

BARBARA

We're together. That's all that matters. Now, why don't you sit down and relax. I'll get things together and make a special meal. *(RAYMOND sits down)* Go ahead and takeoff your shoes, dear. Relax. *(RAYMOND takes off his shoes and socks)*

RAYMOND

(RAYMOND looks around and stares at the palm tree with its one coconut) We're so lucky to find this place, Barb. And it really was a steal.

BARBARA

I was thinking about champagne.

RAYMOND

I could go down to the wine cellar.

MY PARADISE ISLAND

BARBARA

You're resting, dear. I'll go.

(Lightning sounds)

BARBARA (Continued)

Oh, my, it looks like we're in for a storm.

RAYMOND

No worries, dear. I paid extra for the 'no rain, lightning, or wind' option.

BARBARA

You are such a brilliant man.

RAYMOND

I have even better news. We also have a maid to do all the laundry, cooking, cleaning, and she even does sewing if necessary.

BARBARA

When will she be coming here?

RAYMOND

Well, we arrived so late. It's only right she come in the morning. And, dear, I wanted to spend our first day together, alone, on our own piece of paradise.

BARBARA

You're so thoughtful, sweetheart.

RAYMOND

(RAYMOND looks around) It's so beautiful here. I know we'll love it.

MY PARADISE ISLAND

BARBARA

Oh, yes. *(BARBARA looks at the ocean)* My dream has come true. A place of our own, by the ocean, palm tree, no grass to cut, no neighbors to bother us, no bad weather – paradise.

VOICE #1 (O.S.)

Hello? Hello? Does anybody hear me? Hello? I'm right out here. Please. Someone. Find. Me.

BARBARA

Did you hear that?

RAYMOND

Yes. Who do you think it could be?

BARBARA

It sounds like someone's lost. *(BARBARA looks at the ocean)* Look! There's a small boat and what looks like someone in it. Can you see it?

RAYMOND

(RAYMOND gets up and looks) Oh, yes, I think I do.

VOICE #1 (O.S.)

Hello? Please help me. Hello? Does somebody hear me?

RAYMOND

(To BARBARA) Do we have enough for a guest?

BARBARA

I don't think so, dear. I'd like to help out, but it is our anniversary.

MY PARADISE ISLAND

RAYMOND

Do you think it's our neighbor?

BARBARA

It's hard to say. Why don't you ask him?

RAYMOND

(Yelling) Hey, you! Do you hear me?

VOICE #1 (O.S.)

Yes! I hear you! I'm in a bit of a jam. You see I lost my bearings.

RAYMOND

Well, I can help you.

VOICE #1 (O.S.)

I'd be so grateful.

RAYMOND

(RAYMOND points in any one direction) You need to go in that direction. I'm not sure exactly how far, but you'll come to a restaurant. Let me think – oh, yes, the name is Rodger's Family Restaurant. They're terrible for delivery, but I assume their food and service in the restaurant is good. You can tell them we'll never go to their place, but I'm sure they won't care. The manager was a bit of a jerk. *(RAYMOND waves)* BE CAREFUL WITH THAT BIG WAVE! *(RAYMOND and BARBARA stare and then look glum)* I guess we lost our neighbor.

BARBARA

Well, he had a nerve to come here without first asking.

MY PARADISE ISLAND

RAYMOND

You're right, Barb. I'm not going to feel sorry for some guy who thinks it's alright to just come over. I know I would've called and asked first.

BARBARA

Let's forget about him. We still have time to open up our presents. *(BARBARA opens up her suitcase)* Let me go first. *(The suitcase has only a small, wrapped present. BARBARA hands it to RAYMOND)* I hope you like it.

RAYMOND

I'm embarrassed. In all the hustling to pack and move, I forgot to buy you a present. Will you ever forgive me?

BARBARA

You already bought me a present. The most wonderful one you could buy. This paradise! Now, please sweetheart, open the present I bought you.

RAYMOND

(RAYMOND looks over the box) I wonder what it could be. *(Shakes it)* I know what it is! *(RAYMOND opens the box)* I knew it! You really shouldn't have. You're just too generous.

BARBARA

Do you like it?

RAYMOND

How could I not?

BARBARA

I spent the whole year thinking of what to buy you.

MY PARADISE ISLAND

RAYMOND

I'm touched.

BARBARA

So, you like it?

RAYMOND

It's _my_ dream.

BARBARA

I knew it! You never said anything, but I could tell.

RAYMOND

(RAYMOND pulls out a set of keys from the box) Jaguar. What color?

BARBARA

Red, of course. And it's a convertible.

RAYMOND

When is it going to be delivered?

BARBARA

Tomorrow. Or the next day at the latest.

Voice #2 (O.S.)

(BARBARA's cell phone rings. A female voice is heard through the phone's speaker) You should've taken me with you!

BARBARA

Mom?!? Is that you?

MY PARADISE ISLAND

Voice #2 (O.S.)

Who do you think it is? Of course, it's your mom. Your forgotten mom. Left alone as the two of you go off on your adventure. I hope you're happy. Of course, I'm miserable. But why should you care? You never did!

BARBARA

I do care for you mom. You know that. But it's – well, I don't want to be mean – but you know – Raymond hates you, and you hate Raymond.

Voice #2 (O.S.)

That's no excuse. I'm your family. He only came into your life after I changed your diapers, taught you the alphabet, picked you up when you fell down, wiped your nose, feed you, clothed you –

BARBARA

I know mom. But we all grow up and leave the nest. Raymond is my best friend, soulmate, husband for forty years today.

Voice #2 (O.S.)

You've been throwing that in my face for all these years.

BARBARA

I love you mom. But your little girl is grownup.

Voice #2 (O.S.)

Well, la-di-da, you stay with him. I'll go microwave something – like my head – and you won't need to worry about me anymore.

MY PARADISE ISLAND

RAYMOND

(RAYMOND speaks into cell phone) Hey, Mrs. Larson. You'll be glad to know I fixed the microwave before we left.

BARBARA

(To RAYMOND) You're so thoughtful, darling.

Voice #2 (O.S.)

I've set the microwave for five minutes on high. I'm putting my head in it now. I'm pushing the start button. *(Pause)* It's not working!

RAYMOND

It won't start with the door open.

Voice #2 (O.S.)

I can't very well climb inside of the microwave. I know I've put on a few pounds, but still –

BARBARA

We'll send for you to come live with us. I'm sure we have enough room for you. Will that make you happy?

RAYMOND

I'll even paint the spare bedroom your favorite color.

Voice #2 (O.S.)

You would do that for me?

MY PARADISE ISLAND

RAYMOND

Yes, of course. You are the mother of my bride. I know we've disagreed on every subject, thrown things at one another, and both of us – if we're honest – have tried to poison the other one. But let's put that all aside. You come here and live with us. What do you say?

Voice #2 (O.S.)

I'm overwhelmed.

RAYMOND

Is that a 'yes'?

BARBARA

We want you here mom. Please say you'll come.

Voice #2 (O.S.)

I don't believe you're being so nice to me. I am so ashamed of how I treated you. *(BIG BANG)*

BARBARA

(To RAYMOND) What do you think that was?

RAYMOND

The microwave exploded.

BARBARA

How would you know that?

RAYMOND

I said I fixed it. But you know, I have no knowledge of working with electricity. So, my guess is, <u>POOF!</u>, the thing exploded.

MY PARADISE ISLAND

BARBARA

I guess we won't need our guest room for my mom.

RAYMOND

I don't think so, hon. I did feel good she actually apologized for being so mean all these years.

BARBARA

Yes, I was, too.

RAYMOND

Let's get settled. We can unpack. Eat something nice. Drink champagne. Then settle in for a little fun in the sack. What do you say?

BARBARA

You are such a sweetie pie. I love you so much!

[Playwright's note to Director: The mother never actually died by the explosion of what was presumed to be from the microwave over. The "PROOF!" was the gas expelled by the mother after eating too many TV dinners.]

VOICE #1

(VOICE #1 enters) Hey, my name is Jerry. That wave was something else. When did you folks move in? I've been looking for somebody to talk to for years.

RAYMOND

(To BARBARA) You move miles away from civilization. In the middle of the ocean. And it's still not far enough away.

MY PARADISE ISLAND

[Playwright's note to Director: The neighbor, who survived the big wave, is actually the owner of the restaurant. All three become good friends, and a second restaurant is opened on the island, tremendous profits are made, and a mansion is built. All of this was done in three days. It took an extra day because the local labor union went on strike for better meals. Only after offering cooked food rather than cold soup from cans, the union guys finished the job.]

(BLACK OUT)

(END OF PLAY)

IT'S REALLY VERY SIMPLE

Cast of Characters

JACK: Male in his seventies.

GERRY: Monkey.

DUSTY: Horse.

Scene

Living room in an apartment building.

Time

Present.

Playwright's Note

This play was inspired by Dana Sachs. He has been my director, mentor, and friend.

IT'S REALLY VERY SIMPLE

SETTING: *A living room in an apartment building, with a couch, two comfortable chairs with end tables, and a coffee table. A front door, to a hallway, is on stage right. A kitchen door is on stage left. A closet door is wherever the Director deems appropriate.*

AT RISE: *JACK is pacing back and forth. Cell phone rings.*

JACK

(Picks up cell phone and speaks) Hello. *(Pause)* Oh, I'm glad you called back. *(Pause)* Well, Gerry should be here any moment. I'd like you to come over, too. *(Pause)* I'm working on my play. *(Pause)* Yes, that's right, the one about all of us. *(Pause)* What's my problem? Well, I'm stuck. *(Pause)* How far did I get? Um, oh, um, not too far. *(Pause)* Page one. *(Knock at the front door. To CALLER)* Gerry's here. *(Yells toward front door)* Be right there. *(To CALLER)* So can you come over now? *(Knock at front door)* Hold your horses! *(To CALLER)* No, I wasn't talking to you. *(Knock at front door. JACK walks to front door and opens it. To GERRY)* I'll be a Monkey's Uncle. *(GERRY, the monkey, enters. To CALLER)* No, I wasn't talking to you. *(GERRY hangs hat and jacket in closet)* Can you come over? *(GERRY stands with hands on hips, as JACK pauses to listen to CALLER, and then speaks)* Great! See you in a bit. *(Ends phone call. To GERRY)* Are you upset?

IT'S REALLY VERY SIMPLE

GERRY

I was right in the middle of my tanning session. *(Pause)*   You always think that I'm at your beck-and- call.

JACK

Come on, Gerry, don't be so sensitive.

GERRY

Why did you act so surprised when you opened the door?

JACK

You wore your hat and coat.

GERRY

So what?

JACK

We live in the same apartment building.

GERRY

I don't like to go out undressed.

JACK

(Pause) I'm glad you're here.

GERRY

I thought you were going to write the play yourself.

JACK

So did I.

GERRY

We agreed to ACT in YOUR play.

JACK

I know. I know. But I've got writer's block.

GERRY

What's that?

JACK

My creative juices aren't flowing.

GERRY

I guess that's not good for a writer.

JACK

I'm afraid not.

GERRY

(Pause. Sits in chair)   How can I help?

JACK

We should wait for Dusty. *(Pause)* Can I get you something to eat or drink?

GERRY

Yeah. What do you have?

JACK

(Thinking) How about a banana daiquiri?

IT'S REALLY VERY SIMPLE

GERRY

I hate bananas. I've developed more sophisticated tastes.

JACK

(Hears knock at front door and goes to door and opens it) Hey, Dusty, come on in. *(DUSTY enters)* I've got to write this play, and I need help.

DUSTY

What's the problem?

GERRY

(Points to JACK) He said he's a blockhead.

JACK

I said, I've got writer's block.

GERRY

I know what you said. I was just interpreting it.

DUSTY

(To JACK) What makes you think we can help?

JACK

Look, maybe you can, maybe you can't. But right now, I need both of you to give me the inspiration I need.

GERRY

I'm willing to give it a go.

DUSTY

(JACK and GERRY look at DUSTY) I've never written a word in my life.

IT'S REALLY VERY SIMPLE

GERRY

Me neither. *(Pause)* But let's help our best friend.

JACK

(To GERRY) That's the spirit! *(To DUSTY)* What do you say?

DUSTY

(Pause) I've got to sit-down. My hooves are killing me. *(DUSTY sits on couch)*

(Playwright's note to Director: DUSTY, a horse, has a challenging time 'getting comfortable' on the couch)

JACK

I really appreciate both of you coming over to help me. *(Stands)* I'll get something for all of us to eat and drink and be right back. *(Exits to kitchen, on stage left)*

GERRY

(To DUSTY) How're we going to help him write a play?

DUSTY

It can't be that hard.

GERRY

We could get 'writer's block', whatever that is.

DUSTY

Is that a disease?

GERRY

I guess.

IT'S REALLY VERY SIMPLE

DUSTY

Whatever it is, it can't be worse than /

JACK

(Enters from kitchen, holding a tray of appropriate drinks and food for people and animals, including a bale of hay tied with two strings) / Here we go, a nice assortment of stuff. *(Puts tray on coffee table. To DUSTY)* I didn't mean to interrupt. You were saying?

DUSTY

I was trying to overcome my anxiety.

JACK

For what?

DUSTY

I don't know 'what'; I just know: Things have a way of going off-the-rails when you get enthusiastic about something.

JACK

You're being unfair.

DUSTY

I'm being honest.

JACK

Like what are you talking about?

DUSTY

Puppetry.

IT'S REALLY VERY SIMPLE

JACK

What was wrong with that?

DUSTY

You tied us up with strings /

JACK

/ So I could move you, like puppets.

GERRY

(To DUSTY) You're wasting your time. He's not going to admit we always end up on the short end of things.

JACK

You're being ridiculous.

GERRY

(GERRY takes the two strings off the bale of hay and holds them) Let's tie you up and make you a puppet.

DUSTY

Now we're talking.

GERRY

(To JACK and DUSTY, raising one hand) I vote, Jack's a puppet.

DUSTY

(To JACK and GERRY, raising one hand) I vote, the same.

JACK

(To GERRY and DUSTY) This play is about US. We agreed. Right?

IT'S REALLY VERY SIMPLE

GERRY

-

DUSTY

-

JACK

I'm getting a sense of rebellion.

GERRY

(To JACK) Come on, Jack. You said, you always wanted to write a play with a puppet. What could be better than YOU being the puppet?

JACK

(Thinking) You know, you're right. I did say that. It might be a lot of fun. *(Pause)* Okay, I'll do it.

GERRY

I can use these strings (from the bale of hay). *(GERRY ties one string, then the other, around JACK's wrists)*

DUSTY

(Pause) We have a problem.

JACK

What is it?

DUSTY

We need a puppeteer.

IT'S REALLY VERY SIMPLE

JACK

I can do it. *(JACK fumbles with strings in a vain attempt to be the puppeteer and marionette simultaneously, as JACK speaks)* No problem. *(Pause)* Easy as pie. *(Pause. Beat)* Who can we get?

DUSTY

Let me do it.

GERRY

(Pointing to DUSTY's hooves) Do you really think those hooves can hold the strings?

DUSTY

You've got a point.

JACK

There has to be somebody.

GERRY

Obviously, it's got to be me.

JACK

Do you have any experience as a puppeteer?

GERRY

(Pause) Here are your choices: You do it yourself and get all tangled up. *(Pause)* Dusty can try to hold the strings, with his hooves. You know how that will go.

JACK

I guess you're right.

IT'S REALLY VERY SIMPLE

GERRY

Of course, I am.

JACK

Let's try it. *(Pause)* Gerry, you come around in back of me. *(GERRY moves behind JACK, who hands GERRY the two strings)* You move me by raising and lowing one or both strings. Whatever you think makes the most sense. *(GERRY practices by moving one string, then the other, then both strings, as JACK moves his arms in sync)*

DUSTY

Gerry, you're a natural puppeteer.

GERRY

Thanks.

JACK

(Pause) Let's get to work. We need to come up with a clever idea, so I can write my play.

DUSTY

I say we do a Spaghetti Western. It'll be fantastic. *(Pause)* Picture this: I enter the saloon, go up to the bar, and order a drink. *(Pause)* You see, everybody is uneasy, because they've never seen /

<table>
<tr><td>JACK</td><td>GERRY</td></tr>
<tr><td>/ A talking horse /</td><td>/ A talking horse /</td></tr>
</table>

DUSTY

/ No. They've never seen a horse with money.

IT'S REALLY VERY SIMPLE

GERRY

(Pause) Where do you see Jack and me in this scene?

DUSTY

Jack-the-puppet could play the piano.

JACK

I don't know how.

DUSTY

(Laughing at 'joke') You've got strings, like a piano.

JACK

(Pause) I'd still have to learn.

DUSTY

Geez, you could pretend playing.

GERRY

What about me?

DUSTY

Why don't you be the bartender?

GERRY

Are you trying to be funny?

DUSTY

No.

IT'S REALLY VERY SIMPLE

GERRY

You're just trying to reverse the joke about the monkey coming into the bar for a drink.

DUSTY

I never heard the joke.

GERRY

A monkey comes into a bar and orders a drink. The bartender asks for identification. *(Silence)* Don't you get it? Monkeys don't have ID's. *(Silence. GERRY laughs hysterically)*

JACK

Is that the best you got?

GERRY

Let's do a murder-mystery. *(Pause)* Here's a great plot: Everybody thinks that Jack's puppet character murdered Dusty. But I, as the great detective, will discover I was not only pulling Jack's strings, *(Dramatic pause)* but I killed Dusty.

JACK

It does make sense.

DUSTY

Forget the murder-mystery. Why don't we do a sci-fi?

JACK

That's a possibility.

GERRY

They've already done a talking-horse show.

IT'S REALLY VERY SIMPLE

DUSTY
There have been movies about a planet of apes.

JACK
We could do something different.

DUSTY
Like what?

JACK
I'm not sure.

GERRY
I've got it! People expect aliens in a sci-fi. So, we have humans, just like you Jack, come from some faraway planet.

DUSTY
We could make them 'illegal aliens'.

JACK
What are you talking about?

GERRY
(To DUSTY) I'm getting what you're saying.

JACK
Can you clue me in?

GERRY
The sci-fi morphs into a political sage: Republicans versus Democrats. Border security becomes planet security.

IT'S REALLY VERY SIMPLE

DUSTY

Exactly. *(Pause)* We could set up a debate.

GERRY

We should determine all the particulars. You know, the date, place, rules – oh, yeah, we need to pick a non-partisan moderator.

DUSTY

I could be the moderator.

GERRY

No! Nobody's going to see you as anything but a horse's ass, no offense. *(Laughing at 'joke')*

DUSTY

Look, they'll say you were only 'monkeying-around'. *(Laughing at 'joke')*

GERRY

We're really funny. *(Pause)* Why don't we do a comedy?

DUSTY

Yeah, I think that's it. We become the Dusty and Gerry team.

GERRY

No way. I should get top billing.

DUSTY

I'm funnier.

GERRY

Who says?

IT'S REALLY VERY SIMPLE

                    DUSTY

I do.

                    GERRY

Let's leave it up to Jack.

                    DUSTY

No way!

                    GERRY

Why not?

                    DUSTY

You and Jack have this ancestorial thing. He'd be biased.

                    GERRY

We're not doing a political play.

                    DUSTY

Okay, I've got an idea. *(Pause)* Why don't we do a fairytale?

                    GERRY

Now, that sounds really interesting.

                    DUSTY

We could /

                    JACK

/ ENOUGH ALREADY!!! *(To GERRY and DUSTY)* Those ideas are
lame. I'm not going to use them for my play.

IT'S REALLY VERY SIMPLE

DUSTY

You're the playwright. *(Pause)* Look, we've given you plenty of ideas. You don't seem to like any of them. I'm out of here.

GERRY

I'll join you. Let me get my hat and coat from the closet.

JACK

I really appreciate all of your help. *(GERRY gets his hat and coat from the closet, and GERRY and DUSTY exit. JACK sits in his comfortable chair, takes a yellow pad of paper and pen from the nearby end table, and writes and speaks what is being written)* A play in one act entitled, "It's Really Very Simple", by Jack B. Levine. *(Pause. Puts down yellow pad of paper and pen. Sighs.)* It really isn't simple at all. You have to create interesting characters, put them in a situation in which there is conflict, and have your characters struggle to solve the problem. *(Pause)* Sometimes I can sit-down and write almost non-stop, with ideas flowing, until I have a play. *(Pause)* But unfortunately, there are many days I get stuck. Nothing comes to mind, at least nothing creative. *(Pause)* Look, I know the talking monkey and talking horse weren't here. They're imaginary characters to help me get my creative juices working again. *(Pause)* Believe it or not, it helps to think of a lot of possibilities, before you settle on the one you think will work. *(Pause)* But I've learned an important lesson. I just need to let my mind relax a bit, take a break. If I do, I'm confident something imaginative will come to mind. *(Pause)* Well, it's been great sharing all of this with you. I'm going to take a nice walk, now. You can go home, and rest assured I will eventually write a wonderful play for you to see. *(Pause. Stands)* Good night. *(Continued)*

JACK (Continued)

(JACK exits to closet and closes the door. Pause. Loud knocks on closet door, as JACK speaks in sheer panic) HELP!!! I'm locked in the closet!!! Gerry! Dusty! Someone! *(Pause. Beat)* I've got it! *(Pause)* I'm trapped in a small place, alone, without food. There will be tension, heartache, redemption, freedom. It'll be a play to remember! *(Pause. Almost in tears)* Anyone got a pencil?

(BLACK OUT)

(END OF PLAY)

PASS THE AGGREVATION

Cast of Characters

FRANK CURRY: A man in his 50s.

BARBARA CURRY: A woman in her 50s.

ETHAN LAMBERT: A man in his 30s.

LEAH CURRY: A woman in her 30s.

Scene

Dining room.

Time

The present.

PASS THE AGGREVATION

SETTING: *Dining room.*

AT RISE: *FRANK, BARBARA,*
            LEAH, and ETHAN are
            sitting at table.

FRANK

(To LEAH) I'm so glad you and your boyfriend decided to come. It gives us some real quality time together.

LEAH

We wouldn't miss Mom's meatloaf.

ETHAN

You're really a great cook, Mrs. Curry.

BARBARA

You're so sweet, Ethan. We love having you here. I especially look forward to our talks.

FRANK

Don't embarrass the boy, Barbara.

ETHAN

It's fine, Mr. Curry. I'm glad you don't mind me coming over.

BARBARA

How long has it been?

ETHAN

(Looking at LEAH) I've known your daughter for eleven months and two days.

PASS THE AGGREVATION

LEAH

How sweet of you, honey, to keep track.

BARBARA

He's a smart young man. Good chance he'll make something of himself.

FRANK

Well, that's almost fifty Sundays of meatloaf - and good conversations, I might add.

LEAH

(Smiles) Mom and dad, we came to tell you some great news!

FRANK

See Barb! We've sat down for – what is it? – only a couple minutes, and we're about to start one of our great conversations.

LEAH

(Holds up left hand with engagement ring) Well, this handsome man has…

FRANK

(Puts cell phone to his ear) Hold on! My phone is buzzing. *(Pause)* Hey Jerry. *(Pause)* Oh, no, this is a good time to talk.

LEAH

(Excited) What do you think mom?

FRANK

(Still talking on phone) You've got to be kidding. *(Pause)* I've got all the time you need. Tell me the details!

PASS THE AGGREVATION

BARBARA

I think the mashed potatoes need more salt. *(Puts more salt in mashed potatoes)*

ETHAN

(Nervously) I think your mashed potatoes are fine, Mrs. Curry.

LEAH

Mother! Look at my hand.

FRANK

(Talking on phone) Hold on a sec. You've got to tell Barb. *(Hands cell phone to BARBARA)* Here. This is great news!

LEAH

Dad! Look at me. I just got engaged.

FRANK

(To LEAH with no comprehension of what LEAH said) That's nice dear. *(To BARBARA)* Did he tell you yet? *(Pause)* Put him on speaker phone.

BARBARA

(Hands cell phone to FRANK) He hung up.

LEAH

Mom and Dad, please. This is really important.

FRANK

Of course, it is dear. Your mother takes great pride in making the best darn mashed potatoes with her award-winning meat loaf.

PASS THE AGGREVATION

LEAH

I GOT ENGAGED!!!

(Dead silence)

FRANK

You got engaged?!?

LEAH

Yes, daddy. We did. *(Smiles and holds ETHAN's hand)*

FRANK

I got it, too! I love that video game!

LEAH

What?

FATHER

Your mother bought me it as a pre-Christmas gift.

BARBARA

It was nothing, dear.

LEAH

What are you talking about?

ETHAN

I'll take some more mashed potatoes, Mrs. Curry, if you don't mind.

BARBARA

(Adds more salt) I'm so glad you like it, Ethan.

LEAH

I don't know what you're talking about. But can we get back to what I want to talk about. Ethan! Tell mom and dad about our plans to get married.

FRANK

I can't believe it.

BARBARA

Too much salt, Frank?

FRANK

(Excited) Our daughter has finally done it!

LEAH

Daddy, you're going to make me blush.

FRANK

You don't need to be embarrassed. It's all good.

ETHAN

I hope you aren't offended. I was planning on telling you before I asked Leah, but…

FRANK

Why would I be upset? You got engaged. Fantastic.

LEAH

Oh, daddy, I'm so happy you approve.

PASS THE AGGREVATION

FRANK

How about we skip dinner and play the video game Engaged now? *(To BARBARA)* You can reheat all this. Right?

BARBARA

Of course, darling. You go play with Leah's handsome date.

LEAH

He's more than a date, mom!

FRANK

Ready to play, Ethan?

ETHAN

What are we playing?

BARBARA

(Hands iPad to FRANK) You know, I had debated whether ENGAGE was a better video game than DEAD TO YOU!

LEAH

Mom! Dad! *(Slowly with great emphasis)* Ethan proposed and I accepted. We plan to get married soon.

BARBARA

(To FRANK) Oh my God!

FRANK

(To BARBARA) WOW!

PASS THE AGGREVATION

LEAH

So, are you happy for us?

FRANK

Look, we need to set some priorities here.

LEAH

Right! Priority 1, 2 and 3: Talk about the engagement and wedding.

BARBARA

(To Leah) Did you overhear the conversation?

LEAH

Yes, mother, I've heard everything we've said.

BARBARA

Not us. What Jerry said on the phone?

ETHAN

Before we go play whatever, could I have some more meatloaf?

LEAH

(Frustrated but not angry) You touch a piece of meatloaf, buddy, you're going to be sleeping by yourself tonight.

BARBARA

Excuse me, Ethan. I thought you had a good job.

ETHAN

Yes, I do. I work at my dad's law firm.

PASS THE AGGREVATION

BARBARA

Well, Leah said you may be sleeping on your own. So, I started to think you're homeless.

FRANK

What level are you on, Ethan?

ETHAN

Junior partner.

FRANK

I played the video game ENGAGE for twenty-four straight hours and I only got to Level 17. I didn't see anything about Junior Partner. What level is that?

BARBARA

(Scoops some mashed potatoes and puts it on ETHAN's plate) I know your girlfriend doesn't want you to eat more. *(Pause)* I can't imagine why. You look skinny to me.

ETHAN

Thanks, Mrs. Curry. I'm hungry. There's no sense wasting good food.

LEAH

Ethan, sweetheart, tell my parents -

ETHAN

Mr. and Mrs. Curry, your daughter *(Looks lovingly at LEAH as she smiles back)* have decided to get -

PASS THE AGGREVATION

BARBARA

Ethan, oh Ethan, you shouldn't be talking, dear, when you're so hungry. No wonder why you're so skinny.

FRANK

(Typing on iPad) There! *(To ETHAN)* Let's see how good you are at this.

BARBARA

Who wants strawberry shortcake?!?

FRANK

(Excitedly) We'll take the strawberry shortcake in the den and eat while we're playing the video game.

ETHAN

Oh, yes, strawberry shortcake would be great. And that video game will be fun, I'm sure. But can I tell you *(Looks lovingly at LEAH)* our plans?

LEAH

Mom, dad, Ethan has something REALLY IMPORTANT to say. *(To ETHAN)* Go ahead, dear.

BARBARA

(To LEAH) Honey, don't you like the green beans? *(To FRANK.)* You remember Frank how long I stood in front of the cans of vegetables and debated what to buy?

FRANK

Do I remember? Are you kidding me? I thought I would just explode. And come to think of it I just remembered that stupid lady with the crazy hairdo. Do you Barb?

PASS THE AGGREVATION

BARBARA

She grabbed the last can of corn out of my hands!!! *(To LEAH)* Oh, honey, I know you love corn. It was THAT crazy hairdo woman who took YOUR corn!

ETHAN

Gee, I really love corn. *(Realizes his mistake)* BUT green beans are my favorite all-time vegetable. Really. Truly. No kidding.

LEAH

(To ETHAN) You hate corn! *(To BARBARA)* You know I'm allergic to green beans! *(To FRANK)* I'm two seconds away from finding another family.

FRANK

Honey, you're something else. You're always concerned about other families. *(To BARBARA)* As long as Leah wants to find a family to help, I think the Broadman family would be a great choice. What do you think?

ETHAN

Have I met the Broadman family?

LEAH

Forget the Broadman family!!!

FRANK

Oh, right, they're moving. I'd forgotten. Give me a minute and I'll come up with a good family.

PASS THE AGGREVATION

BARBARA

You know, it's wonderful to have a family dinner. We really get to bond together. We're like a seminar on great communications!

LEAH

Mom! You're not seriously talking about THIS family!

BARBARA

Should I be talking about the Broadman family?

LEAH

(Stands holding her glass of water) I want to make a toast.

BARBARA

You're going to make me cry. I know it. You're going to make me cry.

FRANK

(Stands holding his glass of water) Come on everyone. Let's stand for Leah's toast to mom's cooking.

ETHAN

(Stands holding his glass of water) Can we do the toast after we eat. I'm kind of hungry.

BARBARA

(To LEAH) I agree. Feed the starving boy. If I opened up the front door, he'd blow away.

LEAH

As I was saying, let's toast to the engagement of Leah Curry and Ethan Lambert.

PASS THE AGGREVATION

(Dead silence)

LEAH (Continued)
May our lives together be one of happiness for many, many years to come. *(Clinks glasses with ETHAN)*

(LEAH and ETHAN sit)

FRANK
(Looks like a deer in a headlight) Barb, we've been totally rude.

BARBARA
I'm ashamed to admit it, Frank. I'm so sorry.

LEAH
Oh, mommy and daddy, I love you!

FRANK
(To BARBARA) How could you?

BARBARA
(To FRANK) It's not all my fault. You had a part in it. *(To LEAH)* I – I mean dad and me – well, we're ashamed of ourselves.

LEAH
It's okay. I love you both very much. You had other things on your mind. Ethan and I sprung this news on you.

PASS THE AGGREVATION

BARBARA

Don't worry dear. I'm over the lack of salt in the mashed potatoes. And the fiasco of the crazy haired women grabbing that last can of corn. Oh, yes, I almost forgot my meatloaf was overcooked – of course you wouldn't know that. *(To FRANK)* When are you buying me a new stove so I can cook without destroying my award-winning meatloaf?

FRANK

Barb, I told you that money doesn't grow on trees.

LEAH

DAD!!! MOM!!! *(All stare at LEAH)* Ethan and I are going to elope tonight. This will save you a pile of money. You know, no wedding costs.

BARBARA

(Wipes eyes) I'm sorry, dear. I don't mean to cry.

LEAH

Oh, mommy, I thought you'd never hear the good news.

FRANK

(Laughing) Oh, yes, it was good news!

LEAH

Thanks, daddy.

FRANK

Why would you say that, Leah? You didn't overhear what Jerry said. Right?

PASS THE AGGREVATION

LEAH

Jerry? What are you talking about?

FRANK

The phone call, of course. What would I be talking about?

BARBARA

(To LEAH excitedly) You see, Jerry is getting a divorce and part of his settlement is season baseball tickets. Get this *(Pause)* BEHIND HOME PLATE!!! Is that great or what?

FRANK

But we were supposed to call him back in five minutes if we wanted to go to opening day.

BARBARA

That's why I was upset.

FRANK

Right! YOU should have reminded me.

BARBARA

No, dear. I was upset we were teaching our daughter bad manners. You always need to listen to people when they tell you something.

(LEAH opens her mouth)

ETHAN

I'm up for that strawberry shortcake, Mrs. Curry.

BARBARA

Do you want to eat it here or take it in a doggy bag?

PASS THE AGGREVATION

LEAH
Why would we ever want… *(Pause)* I withdraw my question.

BARBARA
No need, dear. First, you may want to leave quickly so you can catch up with the Broadman family before they leave town. Second, you're going to elope or something or other – my memory is not always the best – and you need to go now. Or, maybe, third, you want to get home early to watch the Late Show on television. *(To FRANK)* What time is it? I don't want to miss that show on "Cooking with Pride".

(LEAH motions to ETHAN
to get up so they can leave)

LEAH
Thanks mom. Thanks dad. We need to go.

BARBARA
I would give you some meatloaf to take, *(Looks at FRANK)* but my old stove burnt it. You might want some of the salty mashed potatoes. I know you don't want any green beans. Although your boyfriend needs to put on some weight.

FRANK
Ethan, glad you could make it tonight. We really need to play the video game ENGAGED. I've got to find out how you reached such a high level.

(Kisses and hugs)

PASS THE AGGREVATION

ALL

Bye. Love you. *(LEAH and ETHAN depart holding hands)*

FRANK

That was nice.

BARBARA

You're not angry at me for losing the tickets to opening day?

FRANK

I hate baseball. I only go to games with Jerry because he wants someone who will really listen to him.

BARBARA

It's all about communication. I'm glad we set the right example for Leah and her boyfriend. Do you think they'll ever get married?

FRANK

You worry about the wrong things dear. Let's eat now. I'm starving!

BARBARA

(Sudden flash) Oh, dear.

FRANK

(Very concerned) What?

BARBARA

I'm so embarrassed. I never brought out my new cranberry sauce.

PASS THE AGGREVATION

FRANK
It's okay dear. They seemed a little out-of-sorts. I'm sure they'll get over it.

(BLACK OUT)

(END OF PLAY)

TROUBLING STATE OF AFFAIRS

Cast of Characters

NOAH JACOBSEN: A man in his forties.

ERIC TREMBLEY: A man in his forties.

Scene

An office.

Time

The present.

TROUBLING STATE OF AFFAIRS

SETTING: **An office with a desk and chair, and two side chairs. There is a door. The upper part of the door has a two-way mirror, which the audience is likely to perceive as a window in the door. The walls are bare, and there are no windows.**

AT RISE: **NOAH sits behind the desk, and ERIC sits in the side chair.**

(NOAH opens file on desk and reads to himself)

NOAH

This is quite a report.

ERIC

What you're reading is just a bunch of malarky.

NOAH

That's why you hired me.

ERIC

I hope you're a good lawyer.

TROUBLING STATE OF AFFAIRS

NOAH

You came to me. I assumed you knew of my stellar record of handling cases like this.

ERIC

Yeah, sure, I heard –

NOAH

Ten straight FBI criminal cases. Nine were called 'unwinnable', yet I won.

ERIC

What happened in the tenth case?

NOAH

This is my tenth case. And I'm going to win it. But I've got to tell you something – this FBI report really points the finger at you as the criminal.

ERIC

None of it is true.

NOAH

Let's go point-by-point, and remember I'm your advocate, not your enemy. What you tell me is protected by attorney-client privilege and cannot be disclosed. I need you to tell me the truth and nothing but the truth. If your attorney doesn't know the truth, it makes it all but impossible to pull you out of this mess. *(Looking at papers in file)* Okay, let's start. *(Pause)* A primary piece of evidence is your computer.

ERIC

I never used it.

NOAH

Not even for e-mails?

ERIC

I use my iPhone. *(Pause)* Jimmy Holdings –

NOAH

The tech guy, right?

ERIC

Yeah. He set up my computer.

NOAH

Your fingerprints were found on the keyboard of that computer.

ERIC

I probably touched it. That doesn't mean I turned on the computer. I asked Jimmy to setup my passcode. You should check him out. He probably made the wire transfers from my computer.

NOAH

Let's assume that's true.

ERIC

It's true.

NOAH

I spoke to your chief financial officer –

ERIC

Paul Sullivan –

NOAH

And he said only two people can make wire transfers - you and him.

ERIC

I see your point. Then obviously we now know it was Paul Sullivan who made the illegal wire transfers using my computer.

NOAH

I'll go along with that theory –

ERIC

I don't think it's a theory. It's true.

NOAH

Sure, of course. *(Pause)* But there's still a little problem.

ERIC

What?

NOAH

Who set up the private bank account in the Cayman Islands where the million dollars was sent?

ERIC

How am I supposed to know?

NOAH

It's under your name.

ERIC

Okay, you seem to be struggling here, so I'm going to try to help you along. First, I have never been to the Cayman Islands. Second, I don't even know what bank or account you're talking about. Third, if there is a bank account under my name, it's been set it up by someone else with fake identification documents.

NOAH

(Finishes taking notes, looks at them, and then looks directly at ERIC) Well, that solves the case! *(Pause)* We do have just a tiny, little, insignificant thing I need to bring up. The FBI went to the Cayman Islands and spoke directly to the Bank Manager. He picked your photo out of thirty photos as the person who set up the account.

ERIC

Where did the FBI get my photo? Why is the FBI involved?

NOAH

Wire transfers over State or international borders automatically become an FBI matter, if it potentially involves illegal activity. You have to admit transferring company funds to a private bank account in the Cayman Islands fits that definition.

ERIC

What photo did the FBI use?

NOAH

I don't know where the photo came from. There are plenty of places, like the photo on your license or passport. The FBI would have no problem finding one to use. Who knows? They could've been following you and took a photo themselves.

ERIC

I'm not sure what the truth is. But I know I didn't do it. *(Pause)* What if the Branch Manager is in on the scam with Paul Sullivan? It's possible. *(Pause)* Let me ask you a question. Have I spent one penny of the million dollars? NO!

NOAH

Eric, I'm sorry to say that's not true. According to this document, money has been withdrawn from the Cayman Island bank account.

ERIC

Good! Now you can trace it to Paul Sullivan's account, or you can find out how he spent the money.

NOAH

The FBI did trace the money.

ERIC

Now we're on the right track. You can bring that as evidence to court to prove that Paul took the company money.

NOAH

I wish I could.

ERIC

What's the problem?

NOAH

Do you have bank accounts at United Trust?

ERIC

Yeah. So what?

TROUBLING STATE OF AFFAIRS

NOAH

The FBI found transfers from your Cayman Island bank account to one of your United Trust bank accounts. In fact, it was $277,446.

ERIC

Paul Sullivan had to do that.

NOAH

That exact amount of money was taken from your United Trust account and paid to Royal Luxury Motors, LLC for a new Ferrari F430 Scuderia.

ERIC

I drive a Mercedes – blue sedan. You can find it in my garage.

NOAH

I'm afraid that's not the only car in your garage.

ERIC

You're not going to tell me –

NOAH

Your Ferrari is red. It's beautiful.

ERIC

It's not mine. Someone put it there! This is crazy! I have one car – I told you. It's _not_ a Ferrari. I don't even like red.

NOAH

All the paperwork at the Royal Luxury Motors, LLC shows you purchased the car. The salesman, Doug Hudson, picked your photo out of –

ERIC

Thirty other photos, I assume. *(Pause)* I'm telling you I didn't purchase a Ferrari. Someone impersonated me at the car dealership (Pause.) and probably was the same guy who opened that account at the Cayman Island bank.

NOAH

Do you use your iPhone to take photos?

ERIC

Sure. Doesn't everybody? But I haven't taken any lately. The FBI confiscated it.

NOAH

The FBI found an incriminating photo.

ERIC

What are you talking about?

NOAH

The salesman told the FBI that you asked him to take a snapshot of you in your new Ferrari.

ERIC

That's ridiculous.

NOAH

Then how did the photo end up on your iPhone?

ERIC

How should I know? *(Long pause)* Wait! Let's say Paul bought the Ferrari and asked the salesman to take a photo of him in the car. He then photoshopped it with my face. *(Pause)* Yeah, I know how he got it on my iPhone. Paul borrowed my iPhone. He said his phone was in another suit jacket. He was on his way to New York for a meeting and wanted a cell phone. Paul returned my phone the next morning. That's how he got the fake photo on my phone.

NOAH

That's a lot of ifs.

ERIC

I AM INNOCENT!!!

NOAH

I need to have a credible defense.

ERIC

You're the hotshot lawyer. You bragged about winning nine straight FBI cases that you said others called "unwinnable". So, Counselor, let's see how good you really are.

*(NOAH picks up the file,
leans back in his chair,
and studies the paperwork)*

NOAH

The evidence seems unassailable. An ordinary attorney would just say, "Let's try to get a plea deal." But I told you that I'm anything but run of the mill. So, I'd say it's time for me to prove my worth.

TROUBLING STATE OF AFFAIRS

ERIC

Yeah, that's the spirit!

NOAH

You are NOT guilty! You had NOTHING to do with this crime. All of the evidence clearly exonerates you. Nothing could be clearer. The evidence shows, without any doubt, that I DID IT!

ERIC

(Pause) How could you have done it? You're a lawyer of high repute. We never met until I came here.

NOAH

Exactly. I stole the money. I thought I could blame it on Paul Sullivan and my ex-wife – by the way, they were cheating on me, so I really wanted to 'stick it to them'. But I never expected the FBI to get involved. So, I got arrested. I guess I knew it was over for me. You know, quick trial, long prison term, and years of being confined in a small cell with some other criminal, eating green Jell-O and other horrible non-edible food. *(Sighs)* So, I started drinking and taking drugs – I mean a little more than I usually do – and then, I got this brilliant idea. *(Pause)* I figured the stress and strain of running my business, finding out my chief financial officer was 'doing it' with my wife, going through a horrible divorce, etcetera, etcetera, etcetera – well, it would make anybody go crazy. So, I did. I went crazy. I used my acting skills – honed from an introduction to acting class in college and two community theatre plays – and convinced them I was looney-tunes. Here I am. *(NOAH is pleased with himself)*

TROUBLING STATE OF AFFAIRS

ERIC

Noah, you're right about being here in the psychiatric ward. But you're not here for stealing a million dollars. You murdered thirteen people in cold blood. You're a psycho serial killer. This ward is for the criminally insane. You know, we have these sessions once a month and do role playing. We make up a story and play our parts in the fantasy.

NOAH

You're such a killjoy!

ERIC

I bet you Doctor Jones is going to blame you for coming up with a cuckoo way of finding out who did it. *(ERIC hears someone enter. ERIC and NOAH turn to see JONES)* Oh, here's the doctor now.

JONES

(NOAH moves from the chair behind the desk to the other side chair. JONES sits behind desk) Well, I was watching through that two-way mirror *(JONES points in direction of door)* and heard it all. *(Pause)* So, this is the first time the both of you role played without me in the room. How do you think it went?

NOAH

I'm angry. Eric blurts out that I'm the crazy guy, just when I was going to prove that I'm a super lawyer. *(To ERIC)* You always have to be the 'big shot'.

ERIC

(To JONES) Do I have to be his roommate? He's way crazier that I am. How can I ever get out of here when you stick me with him all the time?

TROUBLING STATE OF AFFAIRS

JONES

Eric, please. We need to stay calm.

ERIC

I don't want to do any more role playing with <u>him</u>. *(Pause)* What about Mike? He's got issues about his dead parents he killed, but at least, he doesn't think of himself as the know-it-all.

NOAH

(To JONES) I wouldn't mind having Mike as my partner. *(Points to ERIC)* <u>This</u> guy's problems are too numerous to list.

JONES

Well, gentlemen, I should be bringing you back to your room. *(Pause)* I think this session went well. There was a good back-and-forth. Good communication skills. Really good.

(JONES leads NOAH and ERIC out of the office.)

(BLACK OUT)

(END OF PLAY)